SNOWSHOE HARE'S FAMILY

by Stephanie Smith

Illustrated by Robert Hynes

Book copyright © 2002 Trudy Corporation and the
Smithsonian Institution, Washington DC 20560.

Published by Soundprints Division of Trudy Corporation, Norwalk, Connecticut.

Book design: Marcin D. Pilchowski
Editor: Laura Gates Galvin
Editorial assistance: Chelsea Shriver

First Edition 2002
10 9 8 7 6 5 4 3 2 1
Printed in China

Acknowledgments:
        Our very special thanks to Dr. Don E. Wilson of the Department of Systemati
Biology at the Smithsonian Institution's National Museum of Natural History for his
curatorial review, and our very special thanks to Robert Hynes for his amazing work
under pressure.
        Soundprints would also like to thank Ellen Nanney and Robyn Bissette at the
Smithsonian Institution's Office of Product Development and Licensing for their help
in the creation of this book.
        The author wishes to thank Linda Ferraresso for her expertise on birds.

Library of Congress Cataloging-in-Publication Data

Smith, Stephanie, 1976-
Snowshoe hare's family / by Stephanie Smith ; illustrated by Robert Hynes.
                p. cm.
Summary: A snowshoe hare raises her family while outwitting dangerous predators.
ISBN 1-931465-16-9 (hardcover) — ISBN 1-931465-15-0 (pbk.)
1. Snowshoe rabbit—Juvenile fiction. [1. Snowshoe rabbit—Fiction. 2. Rabbits—
Fiction. 3. Animals—Infancy—Fiction.] I. Hynes, Robert, ill. II. Title.

PZ10.3.S6548 Sn 2002
[Fic]—dc21

2001049686

Table of Contents

A note to the reader:
Throughout this story you will see words in **bold letters**. There is more information about these words in the glossary. The glossary is in the back of the book.

Chapter 1
The Babies Are Born

It is spring in the **boreal forest**. The sun is setting. Snowshoe Hare hops along a path. She must hurry. She is looking for a safe place for her nest. She is going to have babies.

The forest is filled with tall trees. Snowshoe Hare stops to eat some grass. Snowshoe Hare hears the hoot of an owl. The owl means danger!

Snowshoe Hare hides behind a bush. Her brown fur blends in with the colors of the forest. The owl cannot see her. The owl flies away. She is safe.

Snowshoe Hare stops at a large tree. The base of the tree is hollow. This will be a safe nest. She will have her babies here.

In the night, Snowshoe Hare has four small baby hares. They have brown fur. Their eyes are open. They begin to **nurse** right away. In a few days, the babies will be strong enough to hop around.

Chapter 2

A Forest Home

The snowshoe babies are one month old. Today they join their mother in the forest. They eat leaves and grass. They will come out at sunrise and sunset to eat. They will stay in the den the rest of the time.

Snowshoe Hare's babies follow her on the trail. They eat twigs and leaves. They listen for sounds of danger. They must be careful. **Predators** are out hunting, too.

A snowy owl sits high in a tree. All the young snowshoe hares stay still. The owl cannot see them. Their fur blends in with the bushes.

Snowshoe Hare wants to protect her babies. She runs out from the bush. The owl flies down toward her. Quickly, she hides behind another bush.

The owl cannot see any of the hares. Soon she flies away. The family is safe. They go back to their cozy den.

Chapter 3
Danger!

Fall arrives in the forest. The air is cool. The brown fur on Snowshoe Hare and her babies begins to fall out. Soon their white winter coats will grow in.

One night Snowshoe Hare and her babies hop into the forest. They look for needles and bark to eat. Summer grass still pokes through the forest floor. A young hare nibbles the grass.

One of the young hares wanders away from the others. Young Snowshoe Hare smells the scent of a **lynx**. She looks up from the grass. The lynx is very close!

Young Snowshoe Hare runs. The lynx chases her. Young Snowshoe Hare is too fast for the lynx. She hides behind a bush. Her fur blends in with the colors of the bush.

A squirrel runs down the trunk of a tree. The lynx chases the squirrel. Young Snowshoe Hare hurries down the path. She finds her family. Young Snowshoe Hare is safe again.

Chapter 4
All Grown Up

Snow is falling. Winter is here. Young Snowshoe Hare and her brothers and sister can now take care of themselves. They leave the den to live in the snowy boreal forest.

Young Snowshoe Hare's winter coat has grown in. Her coat is white. She has black tips on her ears and nose. The white fur hides her in the snow.

Young Snowshoe Hare travels along the paths that her mother showed her. They share the same **territory** for a while. Young Snowshoe Hare's large feet help her walk in the snow. She keeps an eye out for predators.

Over the winter, Young Snowshoe Hare finds a mate. In the spring, she has babies. She will show her babies the paths in the forest. She will teach them how to find food. She will protect them from danger.

Glossary

Boreal forest: a region of thick fir and spruce trees. A boreal forest is found in the northern parts of Canada and Alaska.

Lynx: a large animal in the cat family. A lynx has a short tail, long legs, and tufts of fur growing from its ears.

Nurse: to drink milk from a female animal.

Predator: an animal that hunts other animals for food.

Territory: the area where a snowshoe hare lives and finds food.

Wilderness Facts About the Snowshoe Hare

Snowshoe hares are found only in North America. They live in the forests of Canada and Alaska. They also live in the Appalachian Mountains in North Carolina and the Rocky Mountains in New Mexico.

Snowshoe hares are slightly
bigger than cottontail rabbits.
Their hind feet are very large,
like snowshoes. This helps them
move easily through the snow.

Snowshoe hares often live by themselves. When they are ready to have babies, they will find a small den in which to have them. Other times, they will find dens in the ground or safe places under brush.

Other animals that are found in the boreal forest include:

Beavers	Lynx
Black bears	Moose
Ermines	Red foxes
Gray wolves	Snowy owls
Great horned owls	Squirrels